Patsy says it's fun to host. When you are a host and your parents are the guests then you have to wait on them. You should give them a napkin to put their cookies on. Patsy says that learning to be a good host is having good manners. She says that if you have good manners your friends will like you.

Athena

Patsy Says

Patsy Says

written and
illustrated by

LESLIE
TRYON

PLEASE
wait your turn
DO NOT DISTURB

ATHENEUM BOOKS for YOUNG READERS

New York London Toronto Sydney Singapore

For all my
Tuesday-morning
friends,

with love

Atheneum Books for Young Readers An imprint of Simon & Schuster Children's Publishing Division 1230 Avenue of the Americas New York, New York 10020 Copyright © 2001 by Leslie Tryon All rights reserved, including the right of reproduction in whole or in part in any form. Book design by Michael Nelson The text of this book is set in MetaBook. The illustrations are rendered in pen-and-ink with watercolor. Printed in Hong Kong
2   4   6   8   10   9   7   5   3   1
Library of Congress Cataloging-in-Publication Data Tryon, Leslie. Patsy says / written and illustrated by Leslie Tryon. p. cm. Summary: Patsy Pig is determined to teach Ms. Klingensmith's first grade class some manners before their parents come to the Open House. ISBN 0-689-82297-9 (alk. paper) [1. Pigs—Fiction. 2. Schools—Fiction. 3. Etiquette—Fiction.] I. Title. PZ7.T7865 Pat 2001 [E]—dc21 99-89612

Patsy's nose turns red

when she's upset.

When she's *really* upset, her cheeks go red, too. When she's *really, really* upset, her nose, cheeks, and ears all turn red. Patsy gets *really, really* upset when someone does something exceptionally, especially, and unbelievably rude to her, like spilling orange juice and berries all over her brand new sweater.

On Monday morning, Patsy left the cafeteria and marched directly into the principal's office.

"Mr. Sterling," Patsy said. "Your first graders are **rude!** Before Friday's Open House they must learn some **manners** and I'm just the one to teach them."

"I guarantee that by Friday, if they do as I say, the children in Ms. Klingensmith's class will be as polite as little angels."

"This is a very good idea indeed," Mr. Sterling said.

First thing Tuesday, Patsy arrived in room seven.

"Good morning, class," Patsy sang out. "This week, I'm going to help you prepare for Open House. Today, we will practice **meeting and greeting** guests. I'll pretend to be your guest. Now remember, Patsy says first you must welcome me to room seven. Notice, I'm wearing a hat and coat. What will you do with my hat and coat? I've brought a present, what will you say?"

You can throw your coat in the corner and give ME the present.

Hey! How come SHE gets the present? I want a present.

Wednesday! Only two days left before Friday's Open House.

Good morning Ms. Klingensmith. I'd like to introduce myself. My name is Patsy.

Welcome to room seven, Patsy, we're happy to have you here. Allow me to introduce the class.

"Once again, we're going to pretend it's time for the Open House," Patsy explained. "Yesterday you learned how to greet your guests at the door. Today, my little angels, Patsy says you will practice **introducing yourselves and others**, as I just did."

Hey Sami! Come here, I want you to meet Ryan.

I told you, Zack, NEVER call me Sami. My name is Sa-man-tha!

I'd like to introduce myself, my name is Yoshi. I'm a . . .

I'm not really interested in hearing about you. I'd rather just talk about me.

How-dee, doo-dee

Pat-see, poo-dee!

How do-ooo you-ooo do-ooo? My name is Hope, you may shake my hand.

Huh? Dope? Did you say your name is Dope?

Hope-de-dope! Hope-de-dope! Hope-de-dope! Hope-de-dope!

Sticks and stones may break my bones, but names will never harm me.

Thursday after lunch, Patsy visited room seven again.

"Good afternoon, my little angels," Patsy said. "Today, we will practice the fine art of **serving** cookies and punch at the Open House."

"Now remember, Patsy says first offer your guest a napkin, then a cookie, and say, 'Would you like a treat?' Never fill a cup to the top. If you are being served, remember to take just **one cookie at a time**. The perfect host is **calm and gracious**. Athena, you serve. Zack and Hope, you'll pour. We'll practice with a pitcher of water."

It was Friday and time for the last lesson: Making **pleasant conversation.**

The Open House was just hours away.

Patsy, I'm so glad to have this chance to talk to you. Tell me something about yourself. What's new?

Well, I've been taking tap-dancing lessons. How about you? Are you doing something fun?

"Remember these rules, my little angels. Patsy says you must be interested in the other person. **Ask questions.** Don't walk away when someone is talking. Don't interrupt. Don't talk too much about yourself and **don't talk with a cookie in your mouth.**"

I have a pretty little goldfish in a bowl this big.

That's nothing! I have a HUGE aquarium. I had SIX goldfish but one of them died. It was lying on top of the water, like this.

Hey! Are you talking about me? Are you laughing at me?

Tell me about yourself. Have you always been this ugly?

Here's a question for you: Have you always been this stupid?

I don't think you understand. You must *listen* to Patsy, my little angels. Now, let's review these rules again.

• Listen
• Be interested in the other person
• Ask questions
• Don't interrupt when the other person is talking

It's YOU, sweetie, who doesn't understand. We don't have to do what YOU say, you're not our teacher.

I GIVE UP!

Patsy took a **time out,** and went to her office to jump on a chair. That's what Patsy does when she's upset and Patsy was really, really upset.

While Patsy was in her office, Ms. Klingensmith called for **quiet time** in room seven.

"Please get out your draft books," she said, "and write about what you have learned from Patsy this week."

Finally, it was **time for the Open House.**

Patsy wasn't upset anymore but she was still very **worried.**
The parents were lined up outside of room seven, just waiting
to go inside. . . .

Welcome! My name is Zack. May I take your coat? Your hat? I'd be happy to hang them up for you.

Mom, I'd like to introduce my teacher, Ms. Klingensmith, and this is our principal, Mr. Sterling, he's our pal. Mr. Sterling, this is our mom and dad.

And this is our brand-new little sister, Julianne, but we call her Peach because she's so soft and she smells so good.

JUSTIN and JACOB'S MOM

JUSTIN and JACOB'S DAD

Here is a napkin
for you. Would
you care for a
cookie? Patsy
baked them.

When it was time for the parents to leave, they each stopped and told Mr. Sterling and Ms. Klingensmith what **a wonderful time** they had.

That's when Mr. Sterling looked at Patsy and said, "The class worked all week long with Patsy, getting prepared. I think that Patsy and the class did **a wonderful job.**"

They all clapped for Patsy.

Patsy went back to her office and wrote

a little note to Ms. Klingensmith's class:

Patsy wrote three words on the blackboard so we would remember them. She wrote the word RUDE, which is what you are if you don't listen and are not nice to somebody. She wrote the word POLITE, which is what you are if you are nice to somebody. Patsy wrote the word RESPECT on the blackboard.